Published by KOALAFUL , a U.S. based company

www.koalaful.com
ISBN: 978-1-942509-07-3
Printed in PRC.

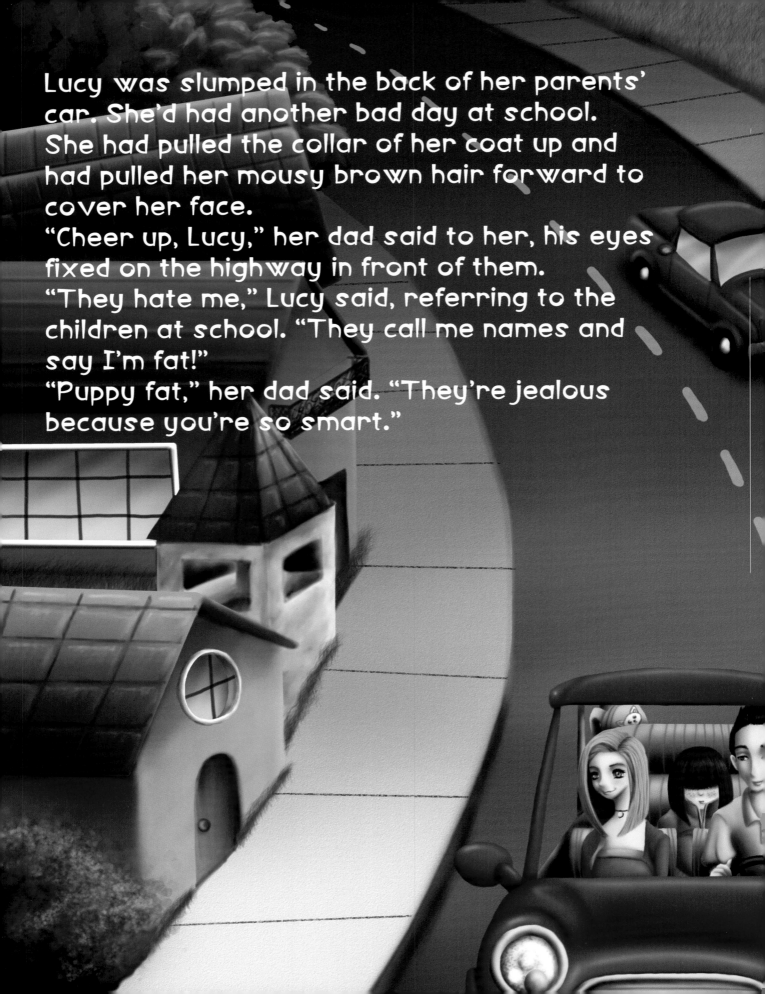

Lucy was slumped in the back of her parents' car. She'd had another bad day at school. She had pulled the collar of her coat up and had pulled her mousy brown hair forward to cover her face.

"Cheer up, Lucy," her dad said to her, his eyes fixed on the highway in front of them.

"They hate me," Lucy said, referring to the children at school. "They call me names and say I'm fat!"

"Puppy fat," her dad said. "They're jealous because you're so smart."

Lucy made a face at her dad. Why did he think saying "puppy fat" would make her feel better? *Fat is fat*, she thought. She was smart but it didn't do her any good. She sat at the back of the class too scared to say anything in case the other kids teased her.

"They say I have cooties because my skin is so horrible and they won't play with me in case they catch it," Lucy said sadly.

"They're just being silly," her dad said. "It's just eczema. It will clear up eventually."

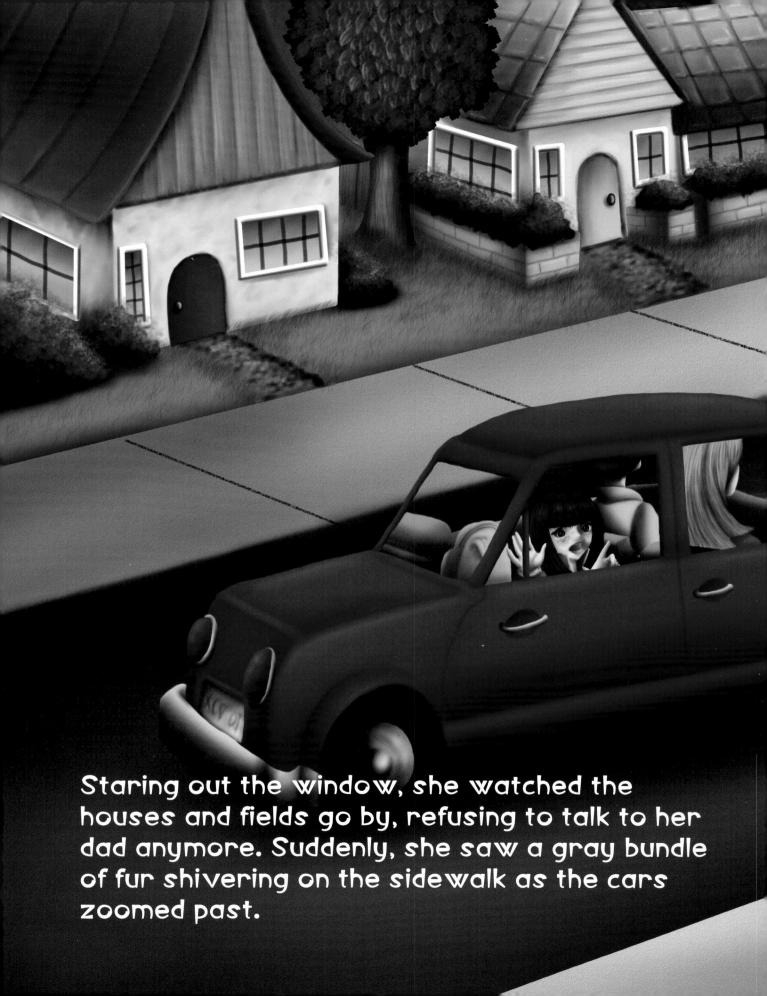

Staring out the window, she watched the houses and fields go by, refusing to talk to her dad anymore. Suddenly, she saw a gray bundle of fur shivering on the sidewalk as the cars zoomed past.

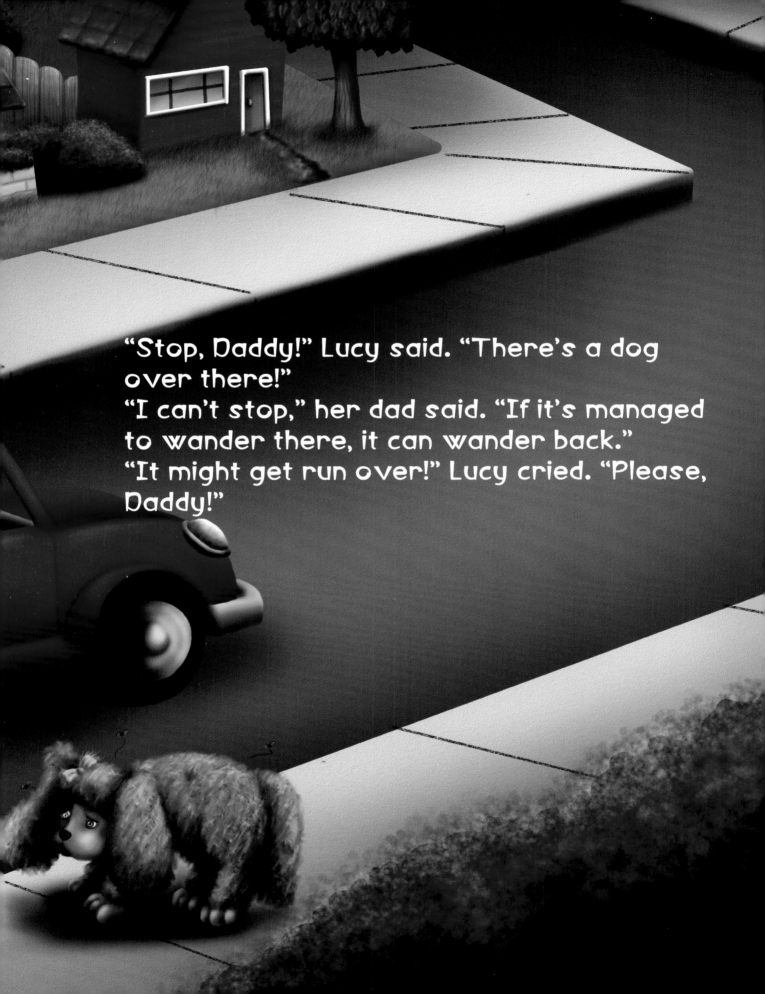

"Stop, Daddy!" Lucy said. "There's a dog over there!"

"I can't stop," her dad said. "If it's managed to wander there, it can wander back."

"It might get run over!" Lucy cried. "Please, Daddy!"

Her dad grumbled as he pulled over to the side of the road.

As soon as the car had stopped, Lucy unfastened her seatbelt and jumped out of the car. She raced toward the dog.

"Lucy!" her dad shouted. "Don't run off!"

Lucy stopped.

"Here doggy, doggy, doggy," she shouted, patting her hand against her legs. "Come on, doggy!"

The dog looked up at her and came trotting over.

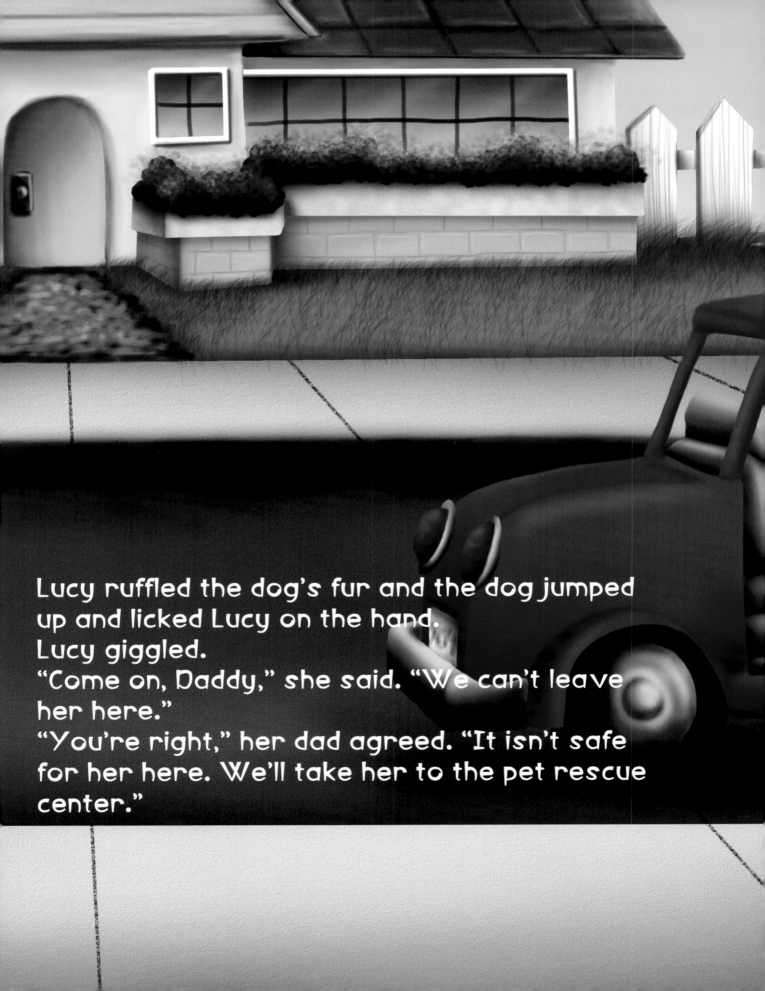

Lucy ruffled the dog's fur and the dog jumped up and licked Lucy on the hand.

Lucy giggled.

"Come on, Daddy," she said. "We can't leave her here."

"You're right," her dad agreed. "It isn't safe for her here. We'll take her to the pet rescue center."

Her dad opened the door and Lucy and the dog jumped into the backseat. Lucy fastened her seatbelt as her dad started the car and drove away. They dropped the dog off at the rescue center and Lucy left feeling concerned about the dog.

That night, Lucy made
posters to put up around the neighborhood.
On each poster, she drew pictures of the dog
and wrote the words "Lost Dog" at the top in
big round letters. *Someone will be looking for
her*, she thought to herself.

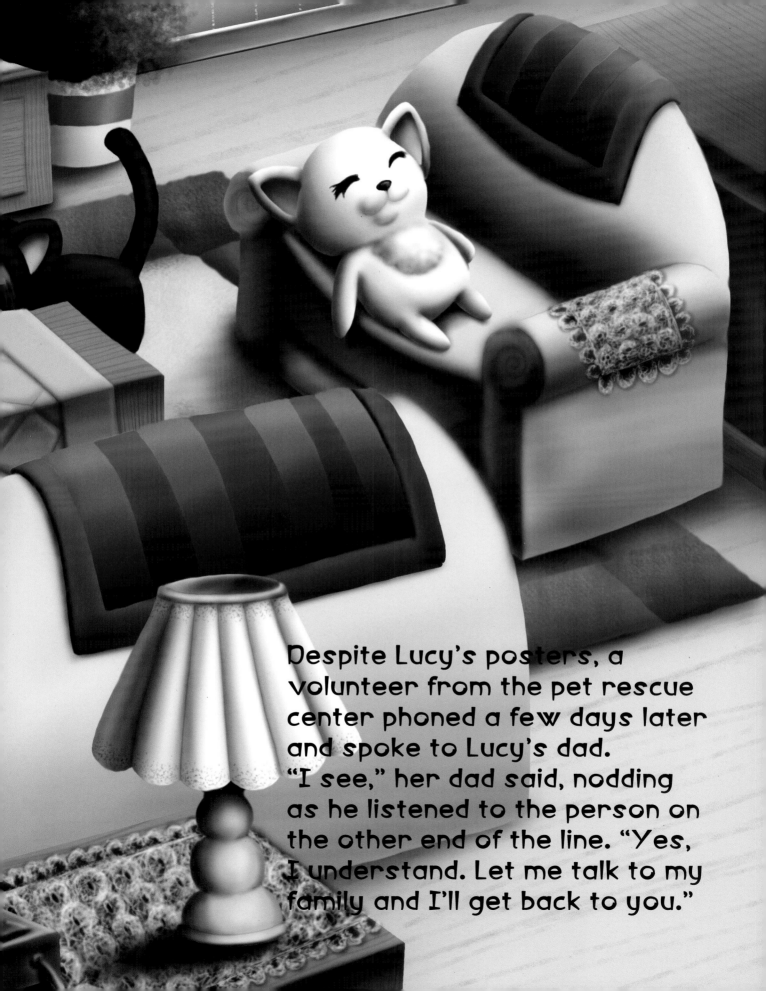

Despite Lucy's posters, a volunteer from the pet rescue center phoned a few days later and spoke to Lucy's dad. "I see," her dad said, nodding as he listened to the person on the other end of the line. "Yes, I understand. Let me talk to my family and I'll get back to you."

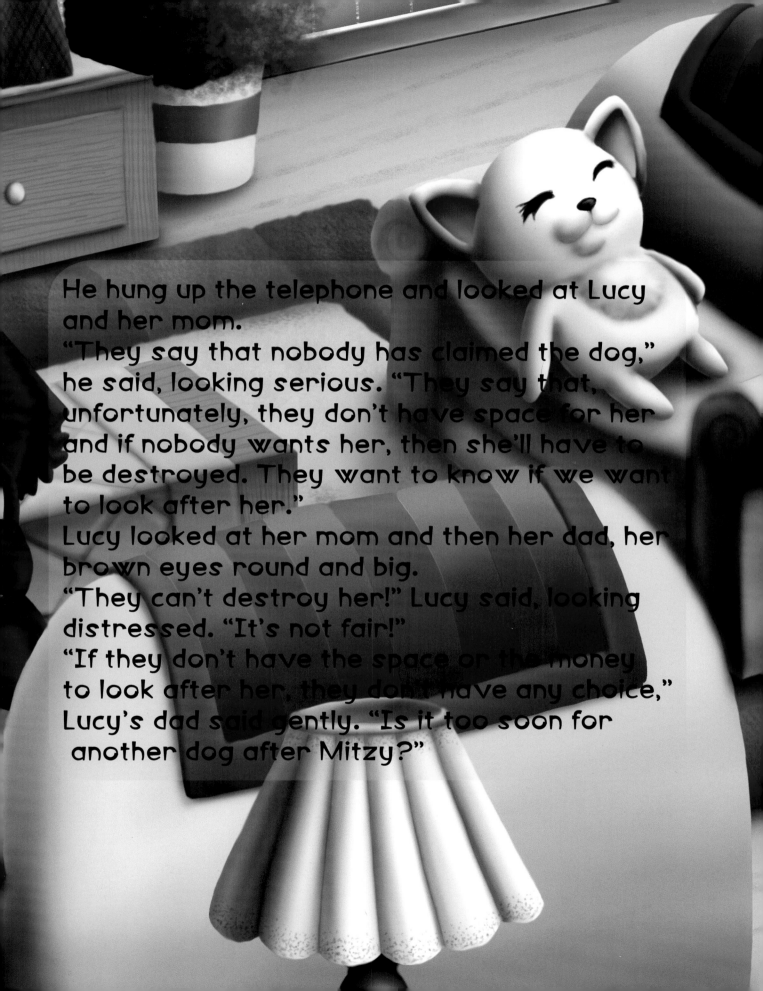

He hung up the telephone and looked at Lucy and her mom.
"They say that nobody has claimed the dog," he said, looking serious. "They say that, unfortunately, they don't have space for her and if nobody wants her, then she'll have to be destroyed. They want to know if we want to look after her."
Lucy looked at her mom and then her dad, her brown eyes round and big.
"They can't destroy her!" Lucy said, looking distressed. "It's not fair!"
"If they don't have the space or the money to look after her, they don't have any choice," Lucy's dad said gently. "Is it too soon for another dog after Mitzy?"

Mitzy had been Lucy's pet and best friend her whole life. Other children made fun of Lucy because of her skin condition and because she was slightly overweight,

but Lucy found that dogs and other animals loved her unconditionally. They didn't care how she looked and they would play with her no matter what, as long as she was kind to them.

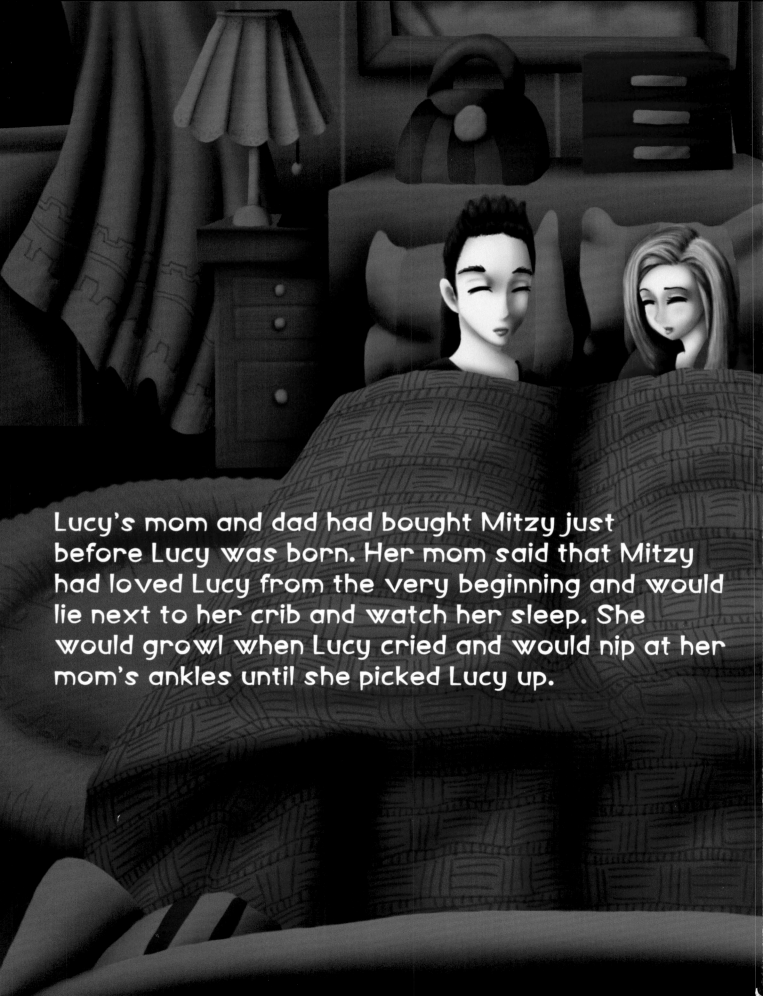

Lucy's mom and dad had bought Mitzy just before Lucy was born. Her mom said that Mitzy had loved Lucy from the very beginning and would lie next to her crib and watch her sleep. She would growl when Lucy cried and would nip at her mom's ankles until she picked Lucy up.

As Lucy grew older, she would throw sticks
and balls for Mitzy to chase and bring back and
would help to feed and groom her. Lucy shared
all her secrets with Mitzy who listened and
didn't judge. Until a few months ago, that is,
when Mitzy died of old age.

"She had a happy life," her mom said, stroking Lucy's hair as she lay on her bed crying.
Lucy had been lonely ever since, but had vowed never to have another dog. She was afraid that she would love it too much and it would leave just like Mitzy did.

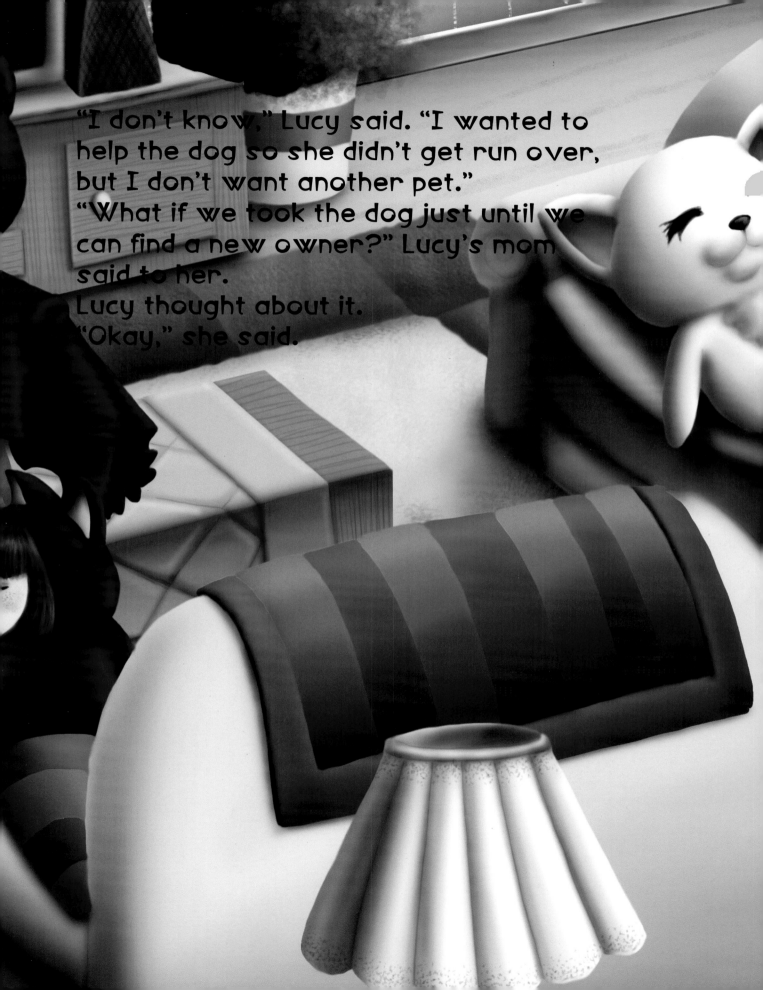

"I don't know," Lucy said. "I wanted to help the dog so she didn't get run over, but I don't want another pet."
"What if we took the dog just until we can find a new owner?" Lucy's mom said to her.
Lucy thought about it.
"Okay," she said.

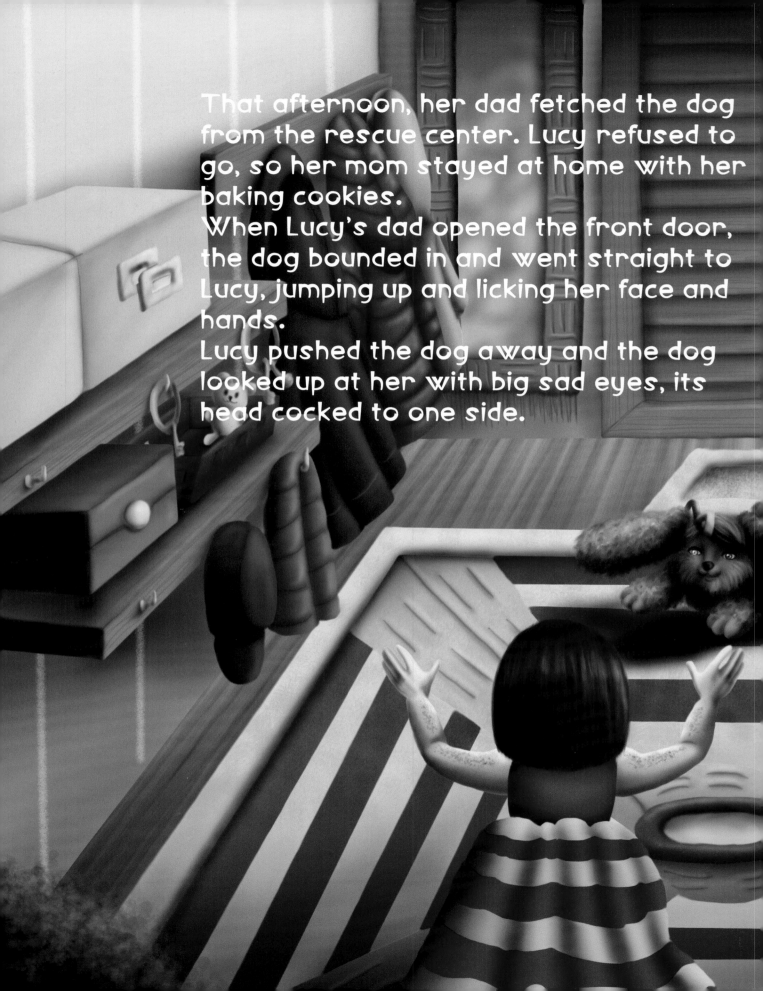

That afternoon, her dad fetched the dog from the rescue center. Lucy refused to go, so her mom stayed at home with her baking cookies.
When Lucy's dad opened the front door, the dog bounded in and went straight to Lucy, jumping up and licking her face and hands.
Lucy pushed the dog away and the dog looked up at her with big sad eyes, its head cocked to one side.

"Her name is Pepper," Lucy's dad told them.
"Stupid name," Lucy muttered.
"How do they know her name?" Lucy's mom asked.
"The lady at the desk said that they called her that because the day after she was brought in someone had written the name Pepper in the dirt outside her cage.

They didn't know who it was—probably one of the staff members playing a joke—but the dog seemed to answer when they said that name, so that's what they've called her ever since."

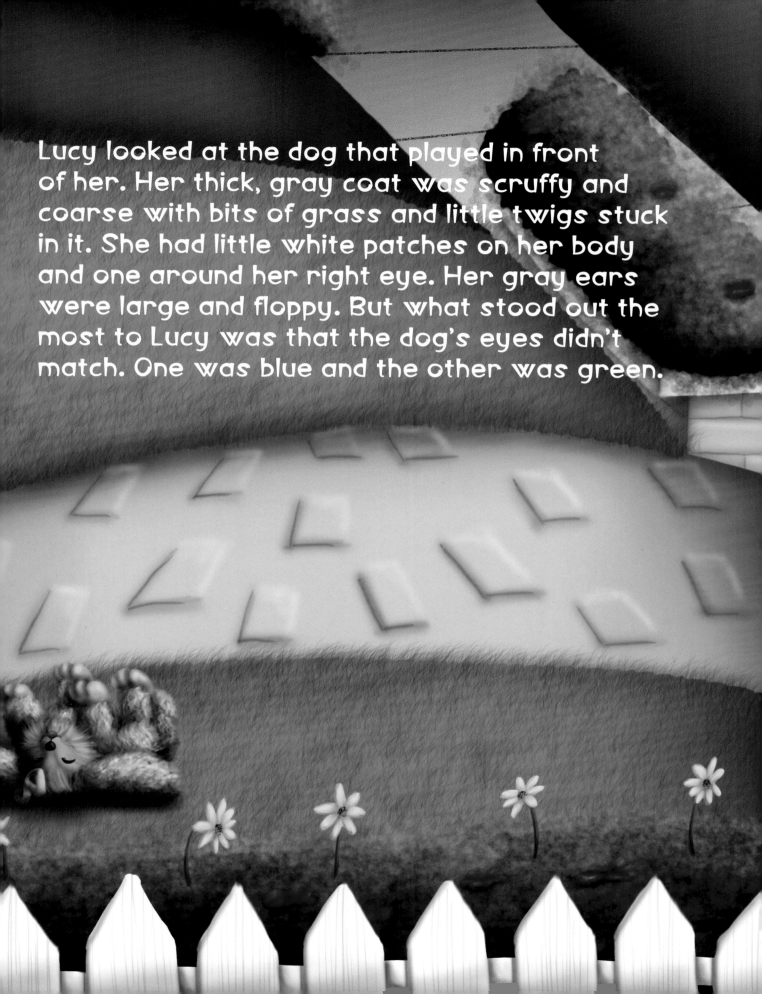

Lucy looked at the dog that played in front of her. Her thick, gray coat was scruffy and coarse with bits of grass and little twigs stuck in it. She had little white patches on her body and one around her right eye. Her gray ears were large and floppy. But what stood out the most to Lucy was that the dog's eyes didn't match. One was blue and the other was green.

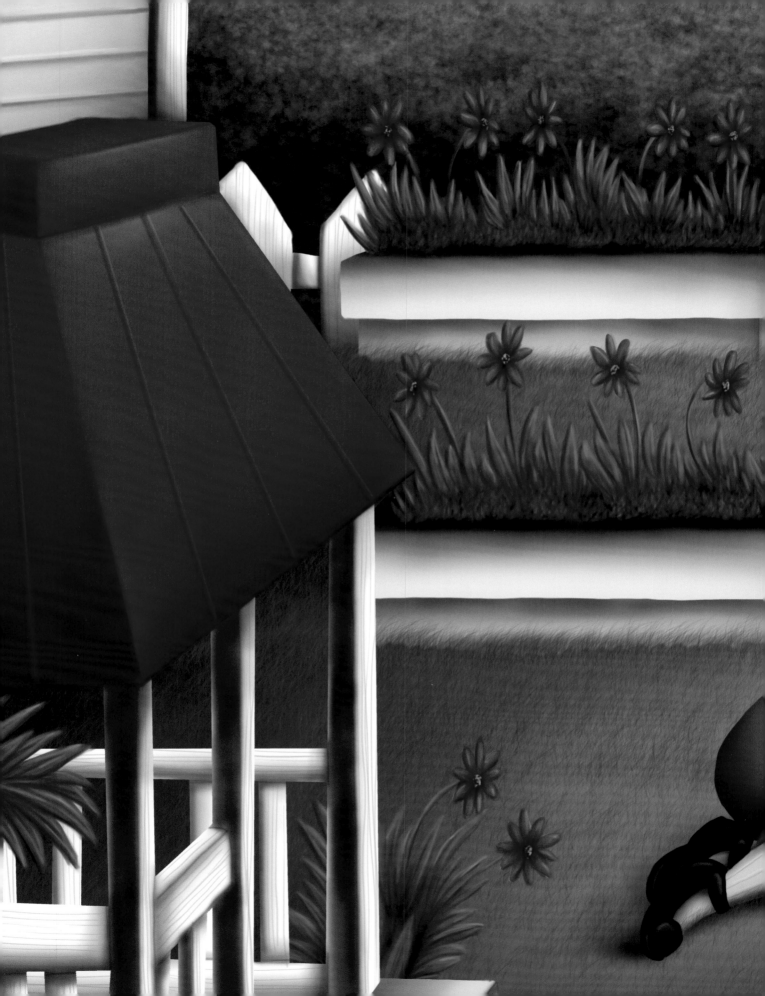

The dog barked once and then lifted a paw up to Lucy.

"She's funny looking," Lucy said, stroking the dog softly. "But then, so am I."

She bent down and rubbed the dog's ears.

"Just don't leave me, okay?" Lucy said.

The dog nudged Lucy with her nose as if to reply.

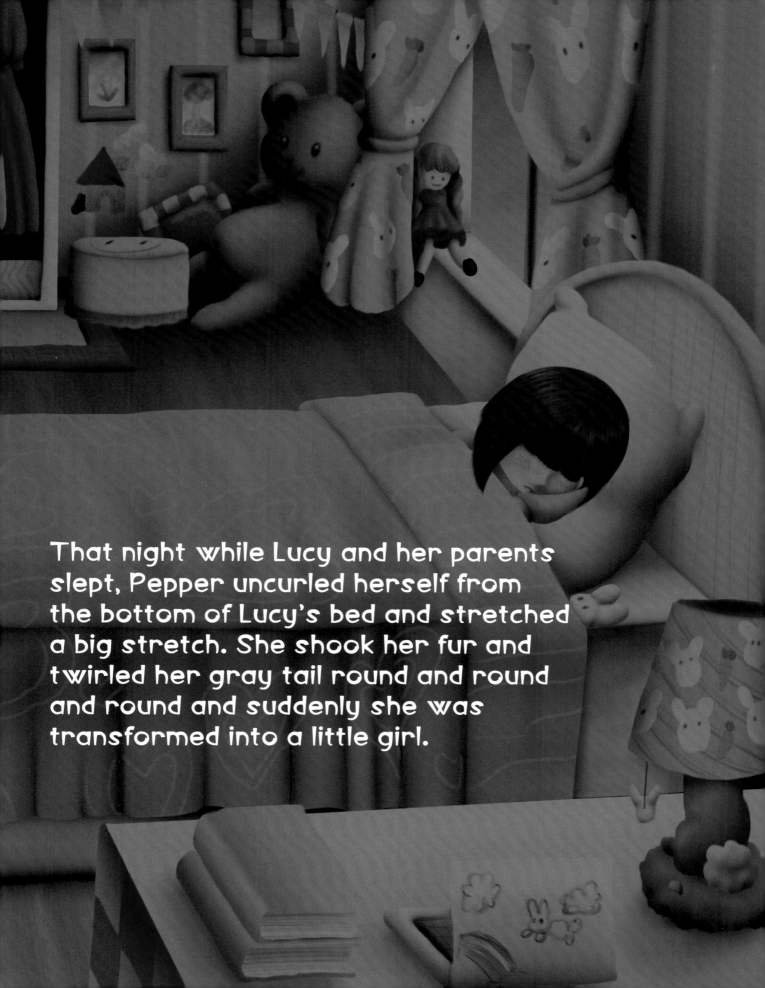

That night while Lucy and her parents slept, Pepper uncurled herself from the bottom of Lucy's bed and stretched a big stretch. She shook her fur and twirled her gray tail round and round and round and suddenly she was transformed into a little girl.

She stayed there for a moment looking at Lucy sleeping peacefully in her bed, her mousy brown hair pulled over her face.

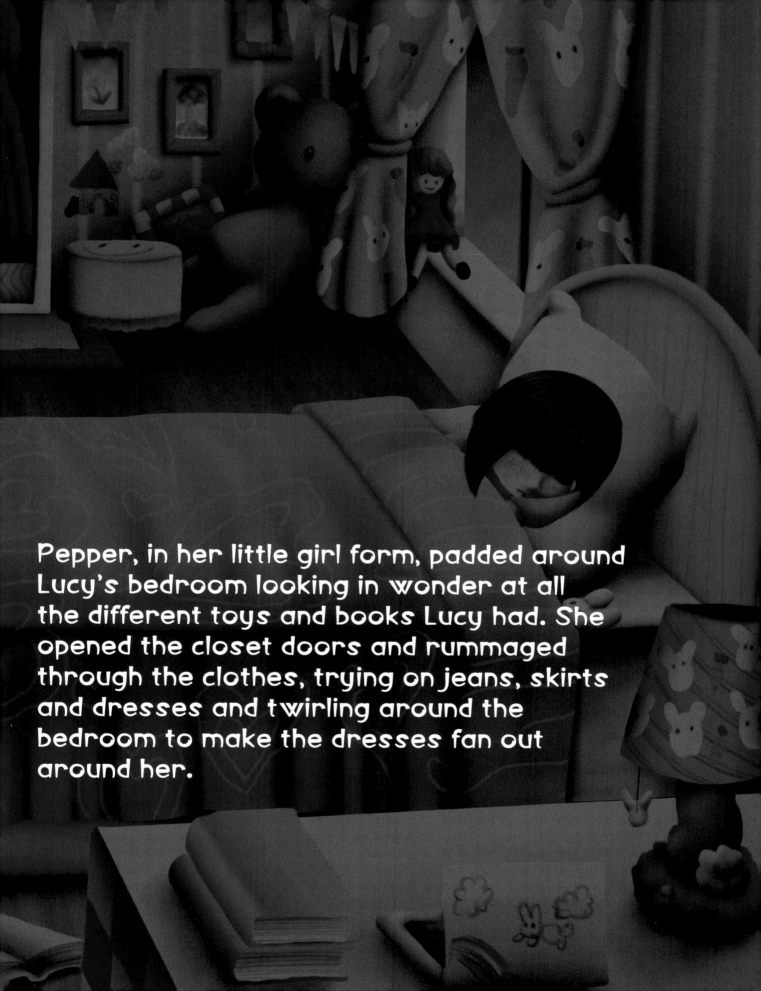

Pepper, in her little girl form, padded around Lucy's bedroom looking in wonder at all the different toys and books Lucy had. She opened the closet doors and rummaged through the clothes, trying on jeans, skirts and dresses and twirling around the bedroom to make the dresses fan out around her.

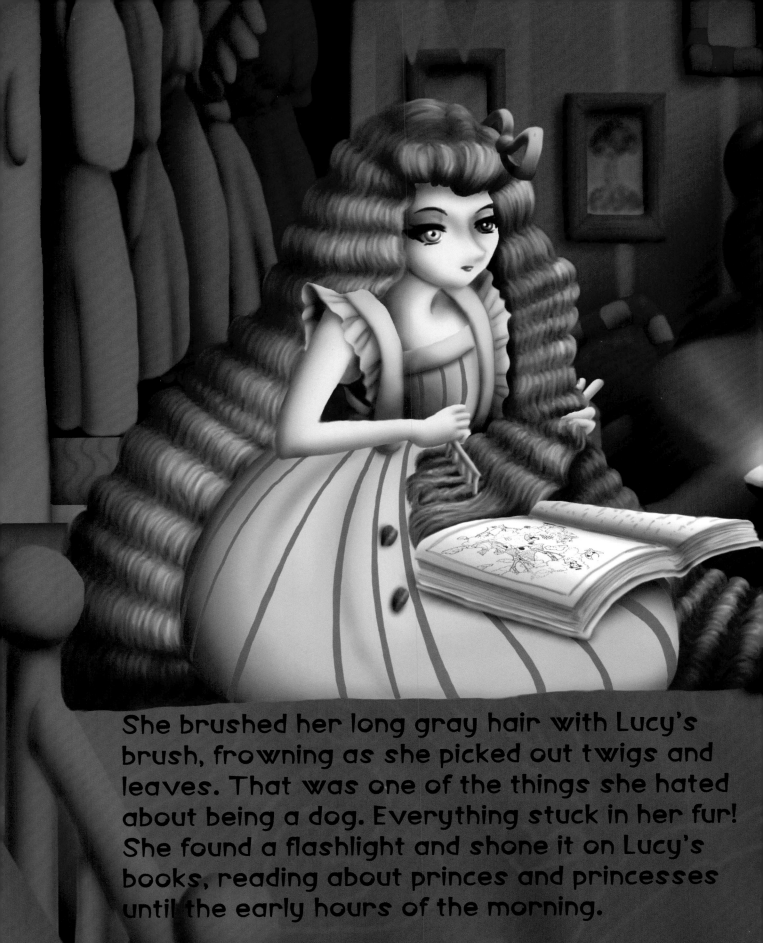

She brushed her long gray hair with Lucy's brush, frowning as she picked out twigs and leaves. That was one of the things she hated about being a dog. Everything stuck in her fur! She found a flashlight and shone it on Lucy's books, reading about princes and princesses until the early hours of the morning.

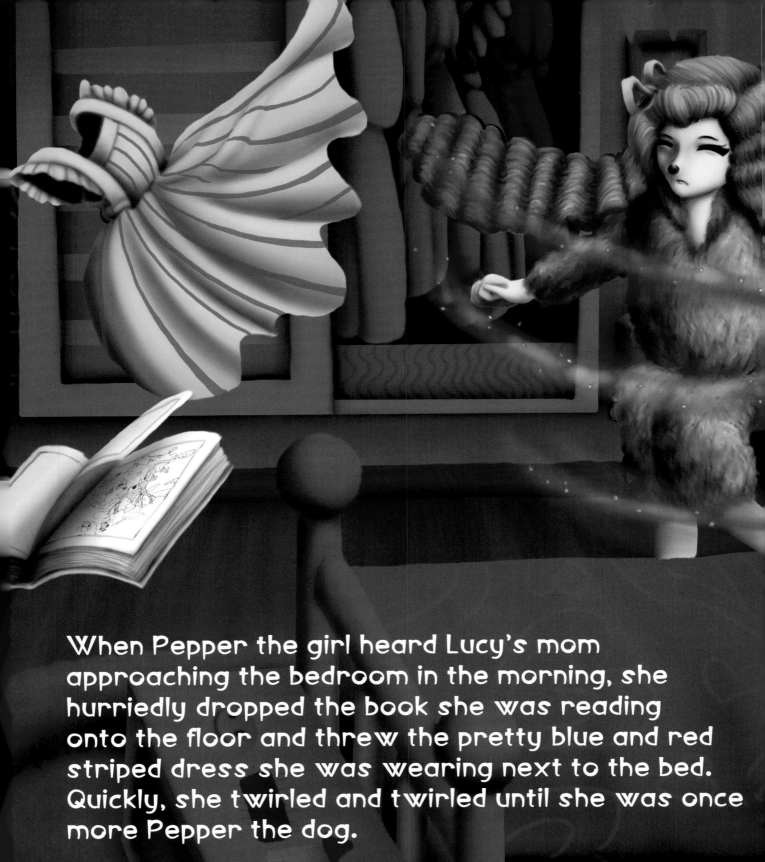

When Pepper the girl heard Lucy's mom approaching the bedroom in the morning, she hurriedly dropped the book she was reading onto the floor and threw the pretty blue and red striped dress she was wearing next to the bed. Quickly, she twirled and twirled until she was once more Pepper the dog.

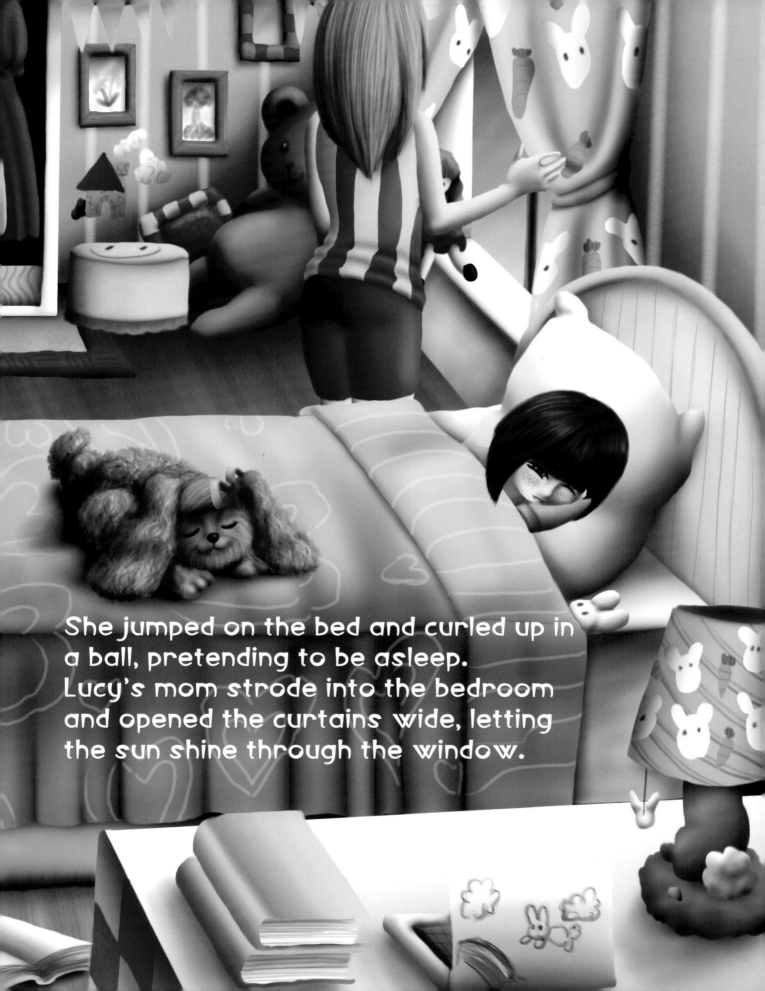

She jumped on the bed and curled up in a ball, pretending to be asleep.
Lucy's mom strode into the bedroom and opened the curtains wide, letting the sun shine through the window.

Lucy sat up yawning and rubbing her eyes. "Really Lucy, pick your things up when you're finished playing with them," she said, putting the book Pepper was reading back on the shelf and picking up the dress that was next to the bed. "You shouldn't really be wearing this anyway. It's a party dress," her mom said to her, hanging it in the closet. She picked up the flashlight and switched it off. "And the batteries will die very quickly if you keep leaving this on all night."

Lucy stretched and her mom looked at her suspiciously.

"Unless you've been up all night reading," she said. "You haven't, have you?"

Lucy shook her head.

"No, I didn't even have the flashlight on and I haven't worn that dress in ages!"

Her mom looked at her in disbelief.

"So it just jumped out of the closet by itself, did it?" she said.

She looked at Pepper, who was still curled up in a ball, and raised one eyebrow before adding, "Or maybe Pepper did it."
A loud snore came from the bed. Lucy and her mom looked at Pepper, who had finally fallen asleep after a long night of exploring. Lucy raised one eyebrow suspiciously. "Maybe Pepper did it!" she joked, and they both giggled at the thought.

The
End